Hairy Hullabaloo

Hairy Hullabaloo

poems by
Richard Stevenson

&

illustrations by
Carla Stein

Wild Man of the Woods Press

First Trade Paperback Edition

ISBN: 979-8-9886342-2-5

Editor and Publisher, Justin Sloane
Cover art © 2024 by Carla Stein
Book design by F. J. Bergmann

Wild Man of the Woods Press

an imprint of Starship Sloane Publishing Company, Inc.
Austin–Round Rock, Texas
starshipsloane.com

List of Illustrations

Table of Contents

Editor's Note

Dear Reader,

Upon first having been introduced to Richard's unique brand of delightfully entertaining and thought-provoking poetry, it was immediately obvious that it was special stuff – in its expert crafting, its subject matter, and its joyous style. You won't find many accomplished poets writing extensively about cryptids and fewer still whose words revel in the kind of great fun that these poems do –

Richard Stevenson

and riotously so! They also provide a sharp and insightful, and at times, even poignant, commentary on human society and our ever-fraught relationship with the natural environment.

Richard once told me that not every editor finds this type of poetry to be quite as amusing as I do. What?! Very serious types may not, I suppose, but then, I think they just might be missing the point. One's literary funny bone deserves tickling through erudite wordsmithing as often as possible! Richard's work is jolly, which is more than enough in and of itself, but it often delivers a message, too. His poetry is just what we need! During the darkest days of the pandemic, he sent along a few batches of his cheerful poetry for publication in Starship Sloane's various magazines, stating that he hoped it would bring a smile to the readers (which I think it did) and to me (which it always did).

Richard has been writing and publishing poetry for many decades now, with much of that poetry having been serious material reflecting on the world around us – but at some point along the way in his creative evolution as a poet, Richard began writing more and more of the fun stuff that fills the pages of this very book, *Hairy Hullabaloo.* I heartily applaud it and suspect that you must as well!

I have enjoyed nominating Richard's work for the Science Fiction & Fantasy Poetry Association's Rhysling Award on a couple of occasions. Richard is retired from teaching English at the college level, is a former editor-in-chief of *PRISM international* and has been the recipient of some major awards, including the Stephan G. Stephansson Award for Poetry, which is bestowed annually by the Alberta Writers' Guild – and he is a member of the League of Canadian Poets. These are serious accolades for a serious wordsmith of fun!

I invite you into a world of cryptid shenanigans, saucy musings, and boisterous hoots! Enjoy your reading.

Postscript: I had finished writing the preceding paragraphs sometime in early October 2023. Not long after, I was informed by Richard's wife of his passing. I felt a wave of sadness that this good-natured and kindhearted human being was gone. And that he would no longer be writing poetry. But Richard's work lives on! I will miss Richard's literary friendship, but I have been given the great honor of bringing this book of his poems to you, and so the teamwork continues. Richard's poetry will cheer you, entertain you, make you think, and warm you as only the blazing hearth of a creative mind can.

Enjoy this book and celebrate the memory and the work of a most gifted poet, whose imagination, in turn, is a gift to us all.

With gratitude,

Justin T. O'Conor Sloane, Editor
December 28, 2023
USA

Yo, Dorothy

Yo, Dorothy, you're right: down home
Kansas is where you wanna be
in a coming zombie apocalypse!

The Kansas Division of Emergency Management
suggested that October be declared
Zombie Preparedness Month back in 2014!

The bill had the backing of the State Governor
and passed! So this is the place
to park an RV or pitch a tent!

You can pack up ahead of tornadoes,
flee the place if need be –
in an RV or tent; rent is cheap.

There is the heating bill in winter, true,
but no self-respecting zombie's about
in the freezing cold of a Kansas winter!

Hey, if you can dodge the cyclones
and not get dropped on some
badass bitch into the bargain, you're good.

Right? You melted the sister;
what's a little twister? Flying monkeys?
The least of your worries! Believe me!

News flash! Zombies are already dead:
You gotta detach their heads
or decorticate the damned things!

Kansas is ready to send 'em packin'
with an array of toxic gasses and
explosives. Zombies blow up real good.

Too many parts to re-assemble.
Hey, you can disassemble zombies
instead of assembling cars in Kansas!

You squished a witch. Now grow wheat
and zap zombies. Kansas will make it
 happen. Maybe turn 'em into tires!

What If Megamouth ...

What if megamouth
had mega cavities,
became a gummer?

Would he hoover up
sea bottom leftovers,
grin a gummer grin?

Would his Mom
mumble through her dentures
See a fith dentith?

What's mega gummer
gonna do without
a mega brain?

Call Dr. Remora,
tell the little dustman
to cement the holes?

Root canals?!
Try riven rivers!
Give him metal posts!

Mega mumbler now
besotted in his suds,
mopping up remains?

Rasta janitor,
night shift hoover hummin'
a salty tune?

Mega gummer spray
comin' your way! Heads up!
Spit and rinse …

He can't Google,
but he can gargle, babe.
Wink wink. Spit and rinse …

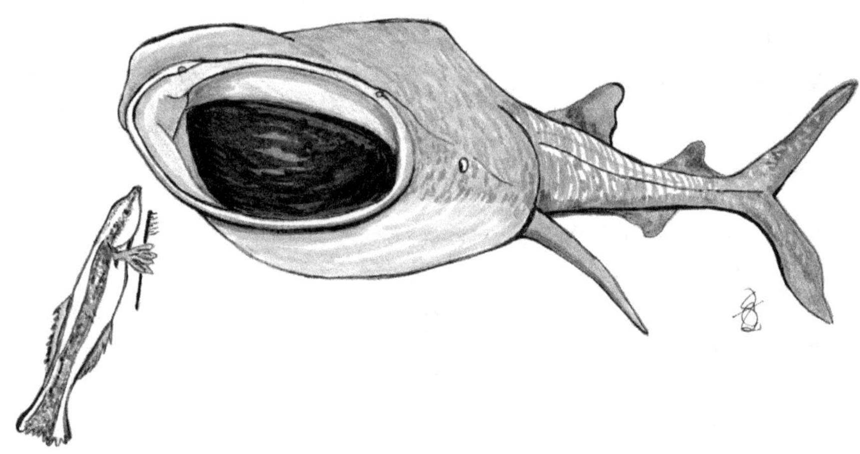

Loup Garou

Loup Garou
howls the got-no-shoes blues
down in the holler.

Sick of ruining
good shirts and waking
up in the zoo.

Apparently scarfed
another *Homo s.* slob
down in the bog.

Woke up in a haze
back in some lion's cage,
hadda make haste …

Showered and shaved,
Wore new brogues and togs
to his *Homo s.* gig.

Sucks bein' him.
Morphodite werewolf doofus,
predator/nerd …

Gotta catch dinner.
Rather take a Mickey Finn,
take the day off.

Even as a human
he's prone to snore –
Satiated carnivore.

Every day
Loup Garou slaps on
the medicated goo.

Trowels away foam,
primps and prepares –
Ladies, beware!

Loup Garou
gets hairy in a hurry,
downright furry!

Hairy schedule too:
nabbin' noble woodsmen
and eating them.

No time for clean-up
when you start to shed,
become human again.

You try it! 'Sno fun
getting your glut,
cleaning yourself up.

Who's got time
for a self! Too much
maintenance, dude!

Smoke Smog Monster

Coming to
a city near you!
Forest Fire Smoke Smog –
amoeboid, phagocytic …
Eats islands, sea, sky!

California
to Canada
east to Halifax!
Gotcha in a smoke vacuole
Gonna make you his!

By pseudopod,
by God,
got you in a clench –
not to mention
his chemical stew!

Chorus
> Boo hoo, baby!
> Don't mean maybe.
> Gonna swallow you!
> Meld molecules
> in his chemical stew!

Come to the smoke
smog monster BBQ!
Eat wood chips
with yer burgers, babe.
Sniff that chemical stew!

Freeze some for yer Mom.
Tell the kiddies
to bring bread knives
to carve through the smog
to and from the school.

Bye-bye Covid.
Got a new bully
on yer block.
Go on and cough!
Breathe in those toxic fumes!

He's alive! He stinks!
Don't matter what you think.
Gonna fumigate
the whole yuppie neighbourhood.
Gonna cover you in soot!

Smoke Smog city!
Gonna turn out the lights!
Smoke Smog monster
ain't droppin' gumdrops.
Got the drop on you!

Chorus
>Boo hoo hoo!
>Got the drop on you.
>Gonna stick to you
>in some filamentous
>cellular residue!

Thirteen Sci-Fi Tanka and Scifaiku

the Bunyip don't need
a genus or species, dude.
can't scare *Homo s.*
circlin' some cement zoo …
Best cop an attitude

Grecian dolphin?
Corfu Island Creature?
or some smiley rubber
boat dock bumper?
think T-shirts, tourist dollars

✳

alas, the moa
has more than a neck in sand –
his four-metre bod
went all-in when it came
to choosing wings or sod

✳

ask anyone!
Orabou tastes terrible!
old camel meat
and Livonian mastiff
even shoe leather tastes better

✳

Loch Ness Nessie
hadda dress up for a date
it had been years
since Nestor put on the dog
or even asked her out

✳

cottonwood seeds fly –
fifties' body snatcher spores
from the great outdoors

✳

hardly a titter
from the Ponderosa pine –
even the grass hot

*

crop hieroglyphics –
alien chemistry clues
or just doodles?

*

giganto hippy
with a passport to our past?
Bigfoot sniffs the rose

*

wife dreams
she's a volvox of eyes –
and all of them can see!

*

cloud-fuzzy contrail
inscribes a robin-blue sky –
stay-puffed on Prozac

*

approach with caution …
may be strange life forms aboard.
ant climbs the orange

*

'Squatch, my hairy man!
you've got a computer now!
can pretend to be bald

Plastic Islands

Plastic islands
floatin' in the deep blue sea …
Plastic islands –
not so dainty houses
for Ms. Virus and me.

Gotta a Big Gulp size
plastic bottle for a home.
Entry's nice and tight,
keeps the fish riff raff out,
allows fungi to sprout.

Fun guys! Doff the togs,
get wet and try to swim
from shore; we gotcha covered!
Covid ain't nothin'. Go on!
Try to swim from shore. PLAS-tic!

Where dry land oughta
reach out to the sea
effluent, bottles,
six-pack beer holder debris,
tampon applicator occupants!

No fun in funky –
We're all sea monkeys
ridin' high on
mountains of debris!
Plastic – so far out to sea!

Hermit Crab's gotta
tampon applicator hat!
stands tall at the helm
of a Styrofoam boat.
Plastic islands! Plastic islands!

A guy could get
a tan way out here –
if not skin cancer
or lesions in inscrutable places,
pock marks on *Homo s.* faces –

if not a little
flush of embarrassment.
Plastic islands
could make plastic homes
if you hauled 'em all to shore.

Coke-bottle houses!
Beer-can bricks, styrofoam homes!
Recycled detritus
Homes for the homeless. Go on!
Collect some green points. Oh yeah!

Recycled debris
for Cleetus Awrightus –
better 'n sewer holes.
Go on! Rent a boat and net.
Scoop all you can get!

DIY –
on-the-fly opportunity.
Plastic islands!
Plastic islands! Free to bag
with bags already there!

Richard Stevenson

Don't Get Pissy, Piscatoré

Don't get pissy,
Piscatoré, cos yer on
a fishin' trip
and catchin' diddly.
Beetcha to 'em, buddy!

Get a load of me!
Two dorsal humps, sinewy bod,
a lanky wiggle
in the water when I oughta
be watchin' my daughter.

Ain't posin' for
selfies with humans.
Got things to do.
Anal asterisk:
Toot toot toodle ooo.

Boat Bottom Roughage

Boat bottom roughage
has got 'im in a slouch.
Old *Homo s.*
just doan wanna digest.
Can't pass gas, boo hoo.

What's a Rasta fish
'sposed to do to get humans
to clean up their mess?
The floating plastic islands
ain't Disneyland to them.

Daughter's got
a plastic six-pack
Tiara, baby!
Don't she look becomin' when
her gills don't get caught.

Richard Stevenson

Eight Sci-Fi Tanka

the Allegewi
like their victims chewy
overweight humans
need not worry or despair
just bring extra underwear

Caddy hadda hunch
the herring school was about
to break for lunch
thought, I'm famished too, why not
pop by for a bite or two?

folks in Penticton
and Kelowna gotta know
when Ogopogo's
Okanagan Follies show
is gonna go virtual

Tazuma's got lots
of room to zoom around
in Shuswap Lake
doesn't need to surface near
Homo s. and his bazooka breed

Bigfoot's feet require
shoes with lights and license plates
the better to see him
when he beats an asphalt path
to scarf roadside blackberries

Bigfoot's nocturnal
his phosphorescent eyes glow
bright red in the dark
that don't make him a demon
or less funky hominid

Abbagoochie
stole a smooch,
played hootchie coochie
emptied his pooch
as soon vamoosed

Kempenfelt Kelly
has cramps in his belly
human and canoe
are too much to scarf or chew
at least for a week or two

Spiffy Ziphius

Spiffy Ziphius,
the Cuvier's Beaked Whale,
cleaves water with
a dorsal fin sharp as
any Wilkinson blade.

Makes rollcall again –
the last of the Ziphius
genus to do so.
Every year he squirts a little
spittle in our eyes as if to say

he ain't no cryptid.
North of the Shetlands
to Tierra Del Fuego,
he cruises the oceans
with a Tupper-tight grin.

Devil's Lake Monster

Legend has it
freshwater octopi
reside in Devil's Lake.
Drowned canoes
of Nakota braves.

Back in the day.
But, nah, the Nakota Sioux
have it the creature
was more like a plesiosaur,
and they tried to appease it.

Fed it slaughtered calves.
You know the story.
Took the long way
around the lake,
hugging the shores.

They didn't have
high air pressure harpoons,
outboard motors;
didn't leave peacock feather
gasoline impressions.

So there you go.
Devil's gone incommunicado
or developed flippers,
Hop-skipped little lakes
left after the drought.

Bought an
evolution ticket out
of Devil's Lake,
waddled over mud flats
to the ocean shore …

Plesiosaur or octopus –
Take your pick. It skipped town.
Vamoosed, scrammed or
scrambled outta there.
Died out or split the scene.

None of the braves
escaped tentacles or teeth.
All bopped or squeezed,
taken to the depths.
Never seen again.

OR

the devil
was a grouper gropin'
in the mud, gasping for air.
Stranded on a mud flat
between evaporating ponds.

Wally What-the-f***
Wallendo succumbed
in a bummer summer
trying to flap himself
between shallow puddle lakes

while sons of absent
fathers stayed their distance
and looked on
a hairy fish with
modified fins tried to walk!

Wally Wallendo
didn't have flippers.
Didn't have
tentacles or teeth.
Didn't have feet.

He had boney plates,
a big boney mouth
that groped at
the prospect of oxygen,
big eyes fixed on the sky.

Pukwudgie

You don't want to tick off
a Pukwudgie, son. They're small
but crafty. Apt to get nasty.

According to the Wampanog,
the Massachusetts changeling
has big ears and a big nose;

is half-porcupine, half troll:
a grey-skinned, three-foot gnome
that can shape shift, become invisible!

Carries deadly poison arrows,
can flock with the sparrows,
alight on a branch and pick you off.

Hey, two or three could push you
off a cliff as an invisible breeze
turned to gust with great gusto and ease.

You'll hear maniacal laughter.
Maybe catch a glimpse of their
Rasta braids. Be *very* afraid.

He can be good too –
if you respect his lands, hand off
the occasional hand of bananas.

Be nice. Leave useful gifts
when you enter Freetown–Fall
River State Forest. Don't drag
any carcasses out but your own.

Richard Stevenson

The Little Devils of Spirit Mound

Eighteen inches tall. Hardly anything
to be afraid of, until they slaughtered
an entire war party set on their destruction.

The Sioux, Omaha, and Otoes respect
them and leave them their mound now.
The little devils have magic arrows!

Earth too: pointy spears of grass
that have grown all over their hidey-holes
now that the place has been made a state park.

Trolls and Gnomes

The Devil's Punch Bowl
near Menomonie, Wisconsin
is said to be their home.

Its naturally-eroded
pillars and spires
a great place for trolls to retire.

Lots of tunnels
and hidey-holes:
a good place for gnomes to hide.

Don't see 'em much anymore.
Musta gone deep underground
to get out of the sun –

avoid *Homo horribilis, Homo s.* II
and his Gorbie outdoorsmen
with their fluorescent vests and guns.

Homo horribilis

Homo horribilis, Homo s. II
certainly deserves a spot in the zoo.
The Urban Man performance piece
got chins of moms and kids waggin',
and that was just an elaborate joke.

A guy chained to a computer and desk
walking about his cage in a suit,
lookin' dapper and professional
with his snapped snappy attaché case.
A good lark. Made a point about cages …

You'll say: we've already got 'em –
lots of spots in lots of zoos.
We call them jails, jobs, schools.
Maybe just set aside a few days
when folks can come and feed him.

Old Tessie

Old Tessie hails from
Lake Temiskaming, Ontario.
(Say that without any snow.)

Does tumble turns
for Turtles and Tim Bits.
I kid you not.

Go ahead and toss
a wiener in the water
with a marshmallow bobber.

You got her!
The world's first
junk-food cryptid!

Think of the shindig
you could orchestrate
with T-shirts and clam bakes!

No crass entertainment
could be crass enough:
Coffee mugs and snuggle bugs …

Plush purple cuddly toys
great for kids
to slobber on.

Matching sheets
and pillow cases –
great for cherubic little faces.

Cryptid games for little kiddies –
better 'n *Free Willy* –
and monster lollypops!

Shoot for the top!
Why not? Great green gobs
of greasy ambergris!

Ice cream and snot
with a cherry on top!
(Nothing with bones or fur.)

Leashes for invisible cryptids!
Sasquatch Ts for Mom and Pop.
Old Tessie books and book marks.

Free rides for the kiddies –
after five. All kinds of ways
to keep them awake and alive!

Old Tessie Photo ops –
selfies with serpent –
Sass perilla by the thimble or drops!

Tess of the Übervilles.
White-toothed as Barney dinosaur,
available in purple piñatas!

Come by car! Come by air!
Come to Old Tessie Fair.
Make your reservation today!

Stay for Tessie's frolics.
Get downright bucolic!
Enjoy our mud ponds and fronds.

Feel waist and wallet loosen.
Feel those dollars drop like autumn leaves.
We have that something everybody needs.

Try our magazine!
Send in your subscription form,
Win a free Old Tessie tote bag!

Richard Stevenson

Shuswaggi's Complaint

Shu- Shu- Shuswaggi
swims all day in Shuswap Lake
A little pasta
just hasta be O.K.
at the end of the day.

He's tired of fish!
Is a senior serpent citizen
with a healthy heart.
Why not a little linguini
or won ton soup for a change?

Homo s. kebabs
would be delectable –
maybe a little
too detectable, but, heh,
he's got all day to work 'em off.

A change of scoff
is what he truly needs.
Some prawns, scampies,
anything that doesn't scamper off
or taste of anchovies!

Hey, he'll show some fin,
flip burgers with his flippers.
Just, please, no kippers,
no trout, no perch, no eels.
He'll even eat wieners and beans!

Richard Stevenson

Bukwus

Bukwus has long hair,
long arms, and a hairy butt,
is anything but
a hippie tending tubers
or über booger in the rough.

He grabs stuff. Has no
manners or graces.
Tears off humans' arms,
leaves 'em strewn about
while he peels off their faces.

A changling too –
not always corporeal.
Sometimes forces a guy to drink
ghost juice to become Bukwus
and prowl the woods with him.

Not your reclusive
'squatch scratchin' his butt
in the all-together.
Not a fair or foul weather friend,
but a sometime furry fiend.

Might as well bring
a rusty blunderbuss to
a laser sabre fight.
You're dead as the dead of night
if you meet a Bukwus.

Yer Bukwus food for
a brute that doesn't clean up
after meals, leaves leftovers
strewn on the forest floor.
B-B-Badass to the core.

Richard Stevenson

Woodsie

Woodsie,
Lake of the Woods'
own cryptid critter
has a crick in her neck,
needs a chiropractor now!

He needs to use
elbows and knees
to get out the kinks.
Get in there and dig
to give her any relief.

Woodsie has a long
flexible neck, it's true,
four flippers, two score
of perfect pointy teeth
she leaves in a glass at night.

She'll leave 'em out
this morning, if you please.
She's down on her knees,
will gum grateful praises
for anyone who can help.

Won't bite when he's done.
Won't howl to kingdom come,
Just purr like a cat
on a mat, hug her thanks
with a flipper round his back.

Bigfoot Boogie

Need big flat feet to
do the Bigfoot Boogie,
stomp dents in the dirt.

Need natty nappy dreads,
fur instead of threads
if yer gonna groove.

Last, but not least, you
need a 'squatch's attitude.
Step lively when you move.

You gotta shake those
knocking knees, move yer hips,
get up to get down.

Yer gonna sweat,
maybe stink a little too,
get the Boogie flu.

Bigfoot has to boogie.
You will hafta too.
Soon be callin' tunes.

The Boogie fever
ain't a dime-a-dance romance,
It'll hang onto you.

You'll sway and prance,
learn to dance
to the Bigfoot blues.

Sinkhole Sam

Sorry, m'am,
Sinkhole Sam's gone on the lam,
don't hang here no more.
Fifteen-foot worms gotta scram
with lots of fishermen around.

Prehistoric worms
got it worse than earthworms too.
Think of what they'd catch!
Prehistoric fish maybe
the size of marlins or sharks.

The worm's dug in deep –
or tunnelled elsewhere it seems.
Don't wanna be fish food
if he hopes to raise a brood
and stick around for eons more.

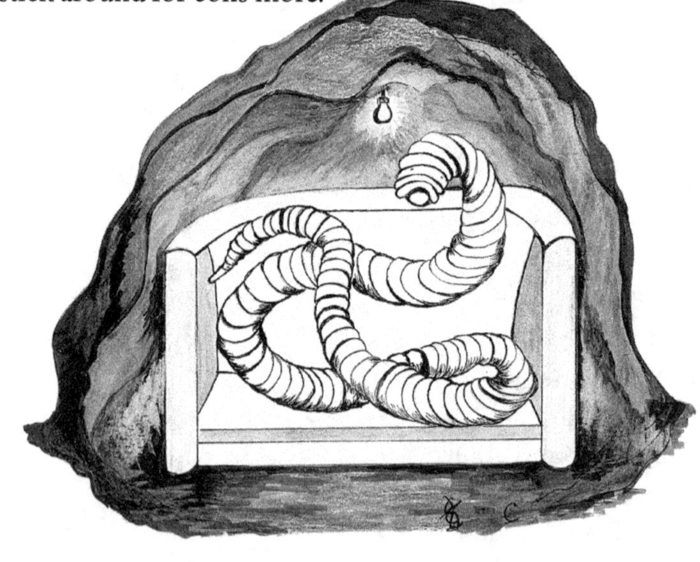

Five Sci Fi-Tanka

you're safe: Mugwump's not
fond of Homo s. kebabs
nor blue burritos
fibreglass ain't fibre
and canoes too hard to pass

can't coax Loup Garou
with blood pudding or sausage
slip him knock-out drops
to get him in your zoo.
changelings don't change diets, dude!

the Rake's not just
some yard or farm implement
he's a monster you
won't catch raking leaves
raking backs with claws maybe …

the Lake of the Woods'
own cryptid critter Woodsie
is kinda circumspect
doesn't do a lot of stunts,
no selfie-with-serpent shots

the Will-o'-the-Wisp –
your strange aerial orbs –
don't stop for Gorbies wearin'
fluorescent gear; they prefer
to stay above the fray

Homo horribilis II

1.
Homo horribilis:
that's what taxonomists
ought to call us.
Homo not so *sapiens* II.
Coming to a theatre near you!

Presenting
extra syllables, little nibbles
at a plot,
the creature time
nearly forgot!

Couldn't get his
shite together
in any place or weather.
Made it snow!
Made it snow!

In his own globe.
The big hand
turned the planet
topsy turvy.
Made it snow.

Captain Zero Mast
cancelled our visas!
We're exempt,
banished to the planet Zenon,
no rudda bruddas.

2.
No rudda bruddas
banished to the planet Zenon
by the big guy.

Someone pushed the button.
(Of course, it wasn't us.)
Cancelled our visas!?

No more
purchasing power!
No more skanky hankies!

Covidiots in space,
we assemble shamelessly
in saucer bars –

without a space buck
to our names!
Without our names!

Adam, get at it!
Start the mainframe
on cloud nine!

Moses, send
a ballistic dove!
Raven, keep an eye on him!

3.
Covidiots in space!
The biggest virus of the bunch
sits down to lunch.

4.
We bought the big one –
not just the family farm –
the whole hominid line!

We sat down to dine,
hadda few animal arse parts,
a few rat-nibbled tarts.

We got the farts,
but had matches, could start
a fire again!

5.
Homo horribilis
bangin' on rusty cans,
twirling bull kelp strands.

Got rhythm back
whacking a lot of old wood,
started arranging it by size.

Big surprise
when we got to oil drums
dropped a few again!

6.

Homo horribilis –
Gonna be a while
re-arranging chromosomes.

7.

Cloud nine, cloud ten …
Hells bells, man – so many clouds …
Which one has our data?

Gonna be a while …
Maybe back on earth the roach
may have survived …

8.

H.M.S. *Dumbfuck*
oughta be our saucer's name.
Ain't gonna claim nothin'.

Nothin' in the name
of any king, queen, mastiff,
bull goose looney.

We've seen the enemy
And the enemy is us.
Yup. Yesiree!
By gum, by gosh,
By golly, by God.

9.
Ate a little crow.
Eat a lot more now.
Don't see any feathers.

No birds here.
Lots of hot stars.
On what would they land?

10.
Saucer bar's old hat.
Ask for a glass of water.
You'd think you asked for
Saturn moon orange juice
or a French Bordeaux.

11.
Homo horribilis,
Canine Copulation Corps,
reporting for duty, sir!

Can't click boots.
Ain't got boots.
Ain't got frenemies.

Got moondust
on my loafers.
Still got soap.

12.
Greatest invention
of all mankind?
Hot running water.

Check!
Still chemically treated.
Gonna have hard, white teeth –

The better to chaw on
whatever cardboard provisions
are stocked aboard this crate.

13.
No rudda bruddas
getting a handle on things.
Digging each other.

Got music, got flicks,
an amazing array of tricks
for plumping potatoes.

Grow 'shrooms in moondust.
Make make-believe omelettes
of goose eggs on balance sheets.

Eat well enough
for spacekateers
on moonbeams.

14.

Some comedian
stuck a Gideon's Bible in my
virtual bedside drawer!

Why not
a Kama Sutra?
I can still dream!

15.

Nearing Zenon now.
Wouldn't you know it?
A sphinx appears.

Got the same face
as Disney's Goofy
sitting next to Donald Duck.

16.

Don't tell me
they've got K-mart here!
Sell shitty goods cheap
in exchange for workers'
life insurance policies.

We're home, boys!
Betcha they have
virtual cigarettes,
play money tokens,
free RV parking.

Jobs too! At shit wages.
No pension plan, but
all the burgers you can eat!

Selma

Seljordsormen –
Selma for short – is Norway's
Nessie-like monster
and loves to swim and cavort
in Lake Seljordsvatnet.

Try saying that with
a mouth full of crackers!
But don't worry.
she hasn't scarfed a human –
yet. Too salty I expect.

Has a croc-like head,
doesn't mind ice cold water.
Used to it, I guess.
Has lots of fish to eat,
baby Selmas to protect.

She has legs to drag
herself outta the water,
but stays circumspect.
Books it for frigid water
should you catch her on the shore.

A cement likeness
gives you something to look at,
but forget the bathysphere!
No scientist has caught her
on camera yet. Too fast!

Maybe she has to
swim fast to survive the cold,
Being warm-blooded.
The fish aren't lollygaggin'
in its dark presence either.

Selma's seldom posed
for candid camera shots.
She hasn't got time
to court the press. Hominid
camera buffs can get stuffed.

Ain't Alien Spores

Ain't alien spores,
but don't let 'em indoors!
They're invertebrate eggs.
A goopy orange soup,
fishy tapioca – but whose?

Kavalinahas,
a small Alaskan village,
woke up to goop at the shore.
It turned the water orange,
suffocated the fish.

Now it's everywhere!
Goopin' up lawns and laundry.
Such a quandary … What lays
so many eggs, and from where?
Don't get 'em in your eyes or hair.

They're everywhere!
Under the doors, in the sink
and drawers. Jellied fish eggs –
Gotta be from space:
nothing here replicates at such a pace!

Richard Stevenson

Folly Beach Monster

Fouling Folly Beach,
a giant monster turned green
baking in the sun.
Shingles of prehistoric scales
ran down its very real back.

Some thought it looked like
a squashed giant pangolin
or monster sow bug.
Nope. An Atlantic Sturgeon,
according to scientists.

Monstrous in size –
an extant prehistoric
boney scum sucker –
rarely seen, seldom smelled,
but here he stinks.

Stank, stunk, towed out, dumped.
Nothing to get hung about.
Shoulda had T-shirts
and coffee mugs made to sell
to locals who stood agog.

So many creatures
we don't know about or see
living lives beneath
the sea, waves drawn back
like coroner's sheets.

We all want to gawk,
we all want a name so we
can consign the beast
to a drawer of phylum
and species, rest easier

knowing authorities
will take away the stink
of death. Bury it in a box
or burn it, so we can toss
its ashes back to the sea.

But knowledge offers
no more than a "know" ledge,
a place to stand when
we dispose of the remains
of monsters we cannot name.

Richard Stevenson

Atmospheric Jellyfish

NASA calls them
Atmospheric Jellyfish –
space debris reflecting
off the northern lights is all.
Good creature F/X though!

I dunno
but I've been told NASA's
told stories before.
Covered recovered saucers and such
down in Roswell, New Mexico.

Maybe aliens
are showing cosmic slides
to the neighbours, eh?
Ever think about that?
Could be a cosmic light show!

"Atmospheric Jellyfish!"
Better 'n knockin noggins
on Zoom with Covid-weary friends.
Don't need to tune in! Just look!
Look up! Look way up!

Captain Kangaroo would approve!
No strings! No puppeteer!
No Rusty or Jerome
hand cramps, crusty dialogue –
just jellyfish cruisin' the cosmos.

Hey, maybe they eat space debris!
Wouldn't that be cool?!
Space jellyfish janitors
cleanin' up our mess! Who'da
guessed 'er, Chester? Who'da guessed?

Richard Stevenson

Six Sci-Fi Tanka

Hungry Grass
ain't lettin' you pass
will eat its fill
on Hungry Hill
the minute you nod off

De Loy's Ape
sat on a crate
mouth agape
propped by a stake
willy to the weather

Could be a gibbon
with tail hidden
or a new world ape!
Go on and gawk! mock away!
De Loy's in a crate either way

Octo-squatch
has eight furry legs
and a furry head
the Basque mountain roads get cold
best wear a Squatch Skin coat.

Old Yellow Top's got
a mop of blonde hair on top
a sasquatch body
Why not a tint and perm?
Mani- and pedicure too?

The Bermuda Beast
jumps so high it can bat
airplanes from the sky.
Shells 'em of human peas,
leaves the rest on the sea floor.

Giant Goldfish

Angler Raphael Bragini
claims he caught a thirty-pound
orange koi carp on a fishing
trip in France. Others claim
the biggest specimen caught in France
weighed an amazing ninety pounds!

Technically possible, if the fish
grew up in a big lake with
lots of nutrients and no predators.
You'd need an aquarium the size
of a house for a thirty-pounder though.
Doubt they make glass thick enough.

Imagine Raphael's surprise when he
managed to drag his thirty-pounder
aboard his little boat. He had
a friend take a picture, then released it.
Local fishermen had tried to catch
that fabled fish for six years!

Raphael must have single-handedly
boosted the tourism industry in France –
fishing that lake in the south anyway.
Imagine he could afford a huge aquarium.
What would he feed his colossal fish?
He'd need a forty-five-gallon drum of food –

Probably every couple of weeks!
And where would he buy a can that size?
And a what colossal price? Impossible!
Of course, he could have faked the photo –
was certainly accused of that,
though no one so far has proven the claim.

Of course, he could have donated the fish
to some French zoo. Or raised funds
for food by allowing kids to ride it
around a swimming pool – if he had one.
Maybe just for a little while –
before the chlorine killed him maybe.

Or he could have cut it into
fish steaks; deep-fried huge chunks
for weeks – assuming goldfish is
not too gamey at whatever age the fish
had attained at that point. Imagine!
All you could eat at some fancy restaurant.

Nope. He let it go; thought the photo
would be enough evidence that such
a giant goldfish lives – in southern France
in an undisclosed southern lake anyway.
Dumped it overboard; watched the locals grin
at their renewed chance of riches and fame.

A giant goldfish. *Should* have saddled
it up for as spin around the lake.
Tied buoys to it so it couldn't dive,
but that would have been cruel, and Raphael
didn't have the stomach for that. Couldn't
get it home alive anyway. Would have been pinched.

Fined an enormous sum, just for being the guy
that managed to catch the fish and settle the question
of its existence. No, throwing it back had been
the better part of valour. He still got the collar
and the picture created a huge stir in the media.
Made believers and doubters that debate to this day.

Giant Goldfish! Thirty pounds or ninety –
enough to sink more than a few bobbers anyway,
and measure happiness in fisherman inches
for another six years. Let the computer geeks
look for fissures in the fish story, prove the photo fake.
Let the foam in beer drinkers' moustaches twitch a bit.

Tahoe Tessie

Tahoe Tessie ain't no cryptid serpent hoser:
she undulates; don't wiggle like a snake.
Prefers trout to polluted, toxic human prey.

She might overturn your boat if you
insist on fishing amid the school
of trout she's chasin' for dinner though.

She has a bad ass reputation, being thirty
to sixty feet long and as big around
as a telephone pole. But, no, she's cool.

Don't wanna hurt anyone. Probably
wouldn't even retaliate if you bounced
a beer can off her pate, but don't try it.

Even prehistoric critters have their limits,
though she probably won't let you get
anywhere near close enough to bop her.

She's camera-shy too. Would rather
retire to her underwater lair beneath
Cave Rock than pose for any shutterbug crew.

Remember: she don't care what genus
or species you want to tag her with.
Don't do tumble turns or interviews either.

She's content to hang in Lake Tahoe
among the myriad of fishes she feeds on,
but don't want any unnatural competition.

The less she has to do with us, the better.
Peacock patterns on the surface from
spilled gasoline don't do it for her either.

So if she pokes her head up too close
to your boat for a *tête-à-tête* with you,
greet her Pepsodent pearls with a smile.

Maybe give her a wave or tip your hat.
Don't start thinkin' of tranquilizer guns
and nets. Fete your own; leave her alone.

Seven Sci-Fi Tanka

the Lake Van Monster –
kin to the Mosasaurus –
snagged a human once
too gamey or maybe he
gave him indigestion.

the Orang Bati
doesn't need a tint or perm
gives two hoots whether
her boobs sag or belly's firm
she's fine with her slow decline

Ishii's got two humps
not saurian saddlebags
or back-pack luggage
Lake Ikeda's Nessie's no
lake camel. Japanese, please!

the Lake of the Woods'
own cryptid critter Woodsie
is kinda circumspect
Doesn't do a lot of stunts,
no selfie-with-serpent shots

Kusshi ain't Nessie
despite the big ad campaign
cute Japanese name
he prefers the coiled-hose pose
to neck stretch and tumble turns

Old Ned doesn't pose
for cell phone shots much these days
Canoe burritos
give him cramps and gas –
Fibreglass too hard to pass

Bessie of Lake Erie
doesn't get the press Champ
and Ogopogo get
Seems she'd rather mind the kids
than grin for top-side idiots

Mike, the Headless Chicken

Headless Chicken Mike
not only walked a while,
he ate through his neck!
Slept, pooped, and scooped
for eighteen months that way!

The axe man had missed
an important nerve which
relayed a message:
Mike, your head went that-a-way,
and so he did too, post haste.

Went lookin' for weeks
until he came back with it
tucked under a wing.
Went straight to a seamstress
to get it re-attached.

It was a hot day
and Mike expired before he
could make his request.
Gurgled and purred but couldn't say
how it was he wished to pay.

Richard Stevenson

Miniwashitu

Miniwashitu
wasn't mini, was he babe?
Stood eight feet tall on hooves;
snapped off my buddy's head
like a stick of celery!

Didn't so much as
belch his approval for the meal –
not that I did either.
Tom and I had been best friends
for better than forty years!

Miniwashitu,
I curse you and all your kin.
You might have a thick
bison-like hide, human hands
and hooves, but I've got grenades!

Hamlet of Lake Elsinore

Hamlet, Monster
of Lake Elsinore,
is his own best ghost,
but, boy, can he snore!

You might not see him,
but walk the shore
after sundown, late at night,
you're bound to hear him roar.

He has a great retinue
of 'bone and bass quakes,
throbbing wah wah wobbling
tones you can hear across the lake,

Make no mistake!
This cryptid could throat sing
with the best Siberian
or Inuit, but has his own thing.

He'll shine at any clam bake
or shimmy and shake rage
you wanna put on for a buck.
Course, you'd need a floating stage.

'Squatches in Saucers

'Squatches in saucers
dropped off near Boston
C'mon! That's gotta
be a fearsome critter tale –
Who'd bought 'er in Boston?

Yet squatches did beam up!
I saw 'em with my own peeps!
Probably thought
Beam me up, Scotty. There's no
intelligent life down here.

He'd a been right too
I reckon this 'squatch
was some kinda Chewbaca
Greys' paid flatfoot flunky
on recognizance duty.

Checkin' on the hominids,
maybe got in some fishin'.
Let us think he's
the primordial primate
knucklin' it in the tuliewumps.

Gig's up, 'squatch baby!
I saw you beam aboard!
I got your number!
Bigfoot's got a big brain!
Bigfoot's got a big brain!

Three SciFaiku

Rochester rat dog
just a shaved guinea pig?
Who'd shave a guinea pig?

Don't mess with Messie!
Lake Murray's dread denizen
ain't no please-o-saur

Philamaloo Bird's
got no knees on his legs,
always lays broken eggs

Richard Stevenson

[Care and Feeding of]
The Flathead Lake Monster

Don't surface much.
You might see me once a year,
though I do runs
of six appearances
when I feel up to it.

Slap tag, tumble turns –
I can put on quite a show
when motivated –
with a nice repast of shrimp
or scampering scampi.

Get tired of trout, eh?
Just give me stomach aches –
and eels are worse.
Make my stomach heave and lurch.
Humans give me pains for days!

You're safe. Too toxic,
Not enough meat on your bones.
Go vegetarian?
Not enough anacaris
to make a decent salad!

Could throw a pizza
like a discus my way.
Toss a teen burger
or bean and cheeze burrito …
Junk food is nice for a change.

Ain't getting fat
on the skimpy scampi here.
Maybe prawns? … Crayfish?
It doesn't need to be a
fancy dish – just fresh.

Tell you what I'll do.
Toss me a good-sized meat loaf
and I'll flash some fin,
pose for cell phone serpent shots,
give you a big cryptid grin.

Mac and cheeze? No thanks.
Too many carbs and calories.
Maybe with tuna –
I could get used to that.
Keto treats are your best bet.

Cheetos and chips
won't make this cryptid flip,
but anchovies? Yes!
Keto burritos? I'm on
my knees for spaniel pets.

The Zaratan

The Zaratan's
giant turtle's shell houses
trees and shrubs,
looks like an island,
a good place to dock, but no –

The island that was
an upside-down monster turtle
nibbled at birds,
the landed gentry, anyone
or anything that landed there.

That why first nations
tribes all call the continent
Turtle Island?
Just so they can invert it,
swallow all the landlubbers?

I like that notion –
It offers a new view of
North America –
an island that can capsize
just like a brigantine can.

Organism 46B

Organism 46B?!
What kinda moniker
is that for a lithe
querulous cryptid
who bumped his noggin
to break ice in Siberia?

I've scarfed enough
intrepid trappers
who braved chilly temperatures
to discover me. The least
the survivors could do
is give me a decent name!

What?! Just cos it's cold
and I live in Lake Vostok,
refused a fish hook or three,
preferred to stay under the ice
and hang near a thermal vent,
I didn't make a dent in history?

Could have been a contender!
The equal of any Ogopogo,
Nessie, Shuswaggi, or Champ!
Shoulda just chomped the legs off
one your intrepid aquanauts
and said I didn't! Who blows?!

Not this fourteen-tentacled
squid-like behemoth, babe!
I did my part just stayin' out of sight
of yer scurvy lot. Coulda scarfed
the lot of you fur-swaddled hominids
and spit out the bones! Man the phones!

'Squatches Got No Watches

'Squatches in the tulies …
'Squatches in the 'burbs …
'Squatches back of my house …
"Squatches on the curbs.

Doan wanna sup with us.
Could care less if we breathe.
Ain't particularly ornery;
would rather take their leave.

'Squatches pickin' berries …
'Squatches catching fish
'Squatches back of my house
'Squatches in the ditch.

Grubbin' with their fingers,
hands wrist-deep in dirt …
Stayin' in a cave now;
wish they had a heated yurt.

'Squatches in the garden
'Squatches in the grass
'Squatches in the culverts
'Squatches in the pass.

Gotta find a safe place.
Gotta get some sun.
Gotta tend their tubers.
Doan wanna get a gun.

'Squatches without watches …
'Squatches with big feet …
'Squatches without worries …
'Squatches fit and fleet.

Will the Real Cryptid Please Stand Up?

Ogopogo,
Nessie, Caddy – fresh or salt
water denizens …

Camel-like snout,
little blunt horns and mane –
the same creature?

Wouldn't that be
a gleeful discovery
and *faux pas* guffaw?

One serpent
to another,
a snigger, a snort.

Hundreds of sightings'
dismissed by snooty profs,
herpetologists:

Water's too cold!
Reptiles prefer hot places
to an ocean or lake!

Zeuglodons are gone!
Plesiosaurs? Puh -lease!
Mosasaurs? All dead!

Eons ago yet!
Get a specimen, drag it
out of myth and mirth –

You had one?!
Half-digested baby baleen
you mean! Doesn't count!

Sightings mean squat
without DNA, you know that!
We deal in facts!

Land a sixty-footer
and we'll talk – Heck,
we'll send a big spool,

help you wind him up
for next-day delivery
to the lab.

Get him on a slab
and check dentition,
silly serpent grin.

Even half rotten
We can check tooth pulp,
extract DNA.

Get one of each?
We'll throw you a parade!
Get 'em alive?

You can write a book
and sell it to a big press
for megabucks!

Snag a movie deal
for a boffo Spielberg
production number.

Don't need videos
or crackerjack stills.
We need evidence!

Okanagan Lake …
Cadboro Bay …
Loch Ness …

Don't care where
you catch 'em, only that you do.
Then we'll dance with you.

You can call the tune.
You can name the critter.
We all come out winners!

White Thang

Is the white thang
a bigfoot or a bear?
Alabama's albino
booger bear ain't sayin' which.
Walks around without a stitch.

Some say he's a bear –
fell into a vat of paint:
a big vat, big bear.
Others say he's a sasquatch,
a birth-marked hominid.

Doesn't matter much
when he slips into the mud
for a steamy soak.
All bets are off when he sinks
up to his chin in brackish bliss.

The Tizeruk

Alaska's cryptid,
the Tizeruk, sports a toothy grin.
Can boast fifteen feet
of moiling coils to impress
all the dizzy Tizzy goils.

When he wants
a midnight snack, he snags
a sailor from a dock
or grabs a local fisherman
straight off a nearby pier.

He'll happily provide
a daytime ride inside his
stomach for the kids.
What's a little acid bath
when you're in a snake at sea!?

G'won, get comfy.
You'll dig the famous water slide,
get to splash around
from his gullet to his tail –
for a long stretch anyway.

Who cares what happens
after a once-in-a-lifetime
super duper ride?
Who cares where the exit is
When it's time for beddy-byes?

Richard Stevenson

Basilosaurus

Basilosaurus –
Zeuglodon, if you prefer –
was an ungulant
but didn't chew his cud
or wear any mammal fur.

Most decidedly
he was a reptile, sir:
a primitive whale
that didn't look like one.
Scarfed his way to fame all the same.

Twelve Sci-Fi Tanka and Scifaiku

Taku He's a 'Squatch
Dressed in top hat and tails.
Furry gentlemen
such as He don't linger long
after dinner and a snog.

Tennessee Wildman
prefers women's company.
If a male stops to
regale him with his wit,
he makes like a tree and leaves.

Huggin' Molly
ain't so jolly and can be
most odiferous.
She hugs you, screams in your ear,
leaves you in a puddle of piss.

sitting in his cave
a sasquatch with a cell phone
watches sasquatch porn

Cynocephali –
dog-head monsters had human bods
and dog face features
Pavlov couldn't condition 'em –
not with dog biscuits or bones

the Quagga lost
half its zebra stripes
then its life
trying to out-pace predators
lions ate up all the lines

to Filiko Teras
only accidentally
tears fishermen's nets
mostly he nibbles bank notes
from tourist's pokes or pockets

vampire Mercy Brown
they say was very composed
didn't rot the way
her younger sisters did
until they staked a claim

first flight to Saturn
Homo s. patrons choose to
hang out in the bar

❋

don't need trampolines
on the surface of the moon –
kids can bounce for free!

Sasquatch staycation –
no one knows better than he
how to maintain
a safe social distance
between hominids

❋

Shuswaggi regrets
she cannot lunch today –
had too much
Homo s.
for breakfast

Igopogo

Igopogo
of lake Simcoe
has a dino bod
and dog head.
Doesn't know
where to go:
lake bottom
or dinner bowl?
Fish or crunchies?
So many munchies!
Schools of fish!
G'won, make a wish!
Fish sandwich
with a soft
dog food spread?
We can do that!
Place your order,
but you gotta
pick it up
in serpent!

Seven Sci-Fi Tanka

How do you please
a hungry plesiosaur?
Feed him fish and chips,
smoked salmon from the shore?
How to say no if he wants more?

Spectre Moose to you,
Inspector Snoop. Not cryptid
so much as irreal –
invisible or fading
from solidity or view

not extinct, just huge –
teratorns on a toot
can snag a V-Dub
off the street and fly with it
through a time portal with ease

'Squatches in saucers
beamed down near Boston
with an ET fleet.
Shoppin' for shoes oughta be easy,
the range of styles hard to beat.

Where are all the shoes?
I heard there was a Shoe Swap
somewhere near here,
the centipede inquired.
I gotta lotta unshewn feet.

Ogopogo knows
when and when not to pose for
human/serpent shots.
Throw him a discus pizza,
he might flash some fin or grin.

T-Rex lives!
Dips humans in butter,
turns them between
scaly lizard claws like
cobs of tasty Taber corn.

Boar Man II

A legend by now, stories range
from reports of a piggy-eyed galoot –
six to eight feet tall – wide as any wide
receiver, carrying a pig tusk
to a husky guy in pig suit,
complete with carved out pig's head.

Get too close, he'll disembowel you
with that tusk, squeaking and squealing
all the while, snorting with pleasure
as he gobbles up your guts, guzzles
your blood like a teenager siphoning
a milk shake. Doesn't even wipe his lips!

Grey beard loon; escapee from some
rubber ranch, or hominid creature
from the Pig Pleiades? Who knows?
Gruff lummox anyway. Best keep your distance.
Better he come to a theatre near you
or smart TV screen than in the flesh.

The Witchita Mountains National Wildlife Preserve
is his hang – lotta rocks, lotta trees. Don't
let him get the drop on you; don't track him
by his spoor or big cloven prints. He ain't
gonna pose for no porcine/*Homo s.* selfie, dude.
You're on the menu: no pork steaks for you!

Cryptid Hodag Kangaroo

Chupacabra,
cryptid hodag kangaroo, drains
yet another ewe!

Didn't anyone
ever tell you it's impolite
to suck insteada chew?

Chupacabra!
What's got into you
besides mammal blood?

Must be nice
to leave the table
without taking your leave.

Rude though. Impolite!
Why not pay for grade A steak,
put it on a plate?

Get used to utensils!
Dab with a napkin, man!
Clean up when you're done!

Don't need drained stoats,
dead mangy old goats,
sheep skin coats!

Get outta here!
Take the fleece, and, please,
brush your teeth!

Orang Mawas

Orang Mawas, Orang Dalam.
yer basic ten-foot Orangutan –
whatever you am! I am Sam,
semi-sentient hominid myself.
Have a banana, man! G'won,
Grab the whole hand from mine.
Have a banana-rama ding-dong
good snackin' time. Here! Some water….
Keep the container; it's re-fillable.
Mind if I take a cell-phone snap?
Promise, I won't snag a bag of your crap.

Bili Ape

Don't just gawk and gape,
my intrepid hominid friend.
Take a picture; it'll last longer!
Leave me to bang on a hollow log,
slog down for a soak in the bog.
Join me, if you like. Bring along
a hand of bananas, some of that
hooch the last crew brought in bottles –
They're fun to blow on when they're empty.
Glad to lend a hand. Whaddaya say?
Two rootin'-tootin' two-fisted simps
suckin' back the brew.
Doin' the rootin' tootin' on the empty bottles!
Eat your heart out, Zamphir!
Manu Dibango's shuffled off, too?!

Aberdeen Wildman

Oops! You got me –
bug-eyed in the bush.
Who's gonna stop starin' first?

I'd introduce myself,
but I gotta vamoose,
grab dinner for the missus.

I assume you don't want
to be featured on
tonight's menu plan.

I'll be off then: 22 skidoo,
yer fellow hominid –
Well, maybe I'm blessed there –

More than you and yer
Double-barrelled friend there
Anyway. Here's my derrière!

No need to fill it with lead!
It'll go where It's led.
To the tuliewumps – and beyond!

Andjing Ajak

Andjing ajak, werewolf of Java,
got the juke joint jumpin' with stories –
big transformation – human to wolf –
and back again. Who's got time
for a shower or costume change
after re-arranging molecules?
I'd stop to refuel on yer lovely dangling bits,
but, to tell you the truth, I'm
a little knackered myself. Could use
a million sheep countdown, a full-sawn log.
Catch you on the flip side, dude.
You might as well forget the silver bullets –
They just go through me while I sleep.
I'm already seeping between scenes.

The Gruagach

A shy, Irish Sasquatch-like hominid
seen all over northern Ireland –
less often in the south, the Gruagach.

Has a wide, high nose, protruding brow ridge,
flattish human-like face and gaze.
A *Gigantopithecus* maybe or Neanderthal?

Nix on the latter: too tall at eight feet.
Bit short for *Gigantopithecus* maybe.
Still, he's hairy, doesn't wear clothes.

Leaves big footprints, builds strange
tee pee like structures. One with
a deer skull found on top once.

Funeral rites? Exterior decorating?
Just how smart is this hominid
anyway? What's under the brow hood?

Generally chooses flight rather than fight.
Eats tubers and berries with his salmon.
Does he laugh when he farts, like a kid?

Does he fart in mixed company? Or belch
his signature to show appreciation
to the missus for a good meal?

He's heard knocking on trees
with big thick, broken bows –
howling in prolonged syllables –

A little makeshift rhythm enroute
to music maybe? A way of signifying
Dad's home from work, has food?

And what does he think of humans?
So downright determined to scoop
up baggies of his fresh poop?!

Strange creatures these. Wouldn't
they rather pick berries or 'shrooms?
Why the cack packs, cement-filled prints?

Don't they get it that he just
wants to be left alone? What?
He's gotta start hammerin' bald domes?

And what's with the buckshot, Holmes?
He's gotta pick flack outta his ass
to get a hall pass in his own home?

Well, here's a particularly gooey and
stinky one for you, Holmes. Kinda goopy
to form into a decent patty. Give it time.

Hope it's full of tape worm cysts or viruses.
Maybe a zoonotic telegram from the past.
Hope the bouquet masks the smell of roses,

fills your lab with a rich brew of fecund
fetid vegetables and three-day-old fish.
Put that on yer dish, under the microscope.

Forget the face mask. Enjoy the bouquet
in both nostrils, there, *Homo s.* G'won
and bless each fetid filthy molecule.

Napa Rebobs

Napa Rebobs – flying robot/monkeys?
Really?! Did I miss something last time
I clicked my heels thrice and chanted
"There's no place like home. There's no place …"

C'mon! After Dorothy put the kibosh
on the wicked witch of the west
all the extra monkeys couldn't find
meaningful work on some other movie set?

Locals say they attack anyone
or anything travelling Patrick Road
en route to the president's doomsday shelter
atop the highest hill in Napa Valley.

Swoop down from the trees either side
of that long and winding road to ward off
would-be biological or nuclear terrorists,
never mind badass witches that just won't melt.

Don't tell me. The wizard behind the curtain
got back to Kansas and applied for the gig
advising the president when to hop on Air Force One's
jet outta D.C., stocked the larder to boot?

Why Napa Valley in a castle on the hill?
Why not some underground bunker or other
nearer to the government's place of business?
Currents carry away nuclear winter winds?

And why a forty-year-old building
inside nineteenth-century ramparts?
Why the smiley face in lights on an outside wall
every Christmas and Halloween?

Something to assure the locals nothing
dastardly is going on behind reinforced walls?
The black helicopters that travel back and forth
are just dropping off the military brass

for a confab over what to do next?
Blast the enemy to kingdom come maybe
or drop a bomb of zoonotic bacteria
or deadly viruses? Trumps a bucket of water.

Or maybe an H bomb that'll leave
buildings standing and melt commies
before they can scurry to their own hidey-holes?
Maybe the president has ruby slippers

and a smoking jacket. Sips tea next to
a slow-burning log or two in the presidential
fireplace while he contemplates his next
State of the Union address. Flips a switch

to turn on the smiley face while he
gets down to the business of running
a tired and grateful nation. Maybe the monkeys
are well-disguised drones with very sharp teeth.

Hominid Stomp Reprise

Well, we're hairy bipedal hominids
with immature egos and active ids
and funky, malodorous teenage kids.
We're hairy bipedal hominids.

—from "Hairy Bipedal Hominid Stomp"
Nothing Definite Yeti (Ekstasis Editions, 1999)

Get down now!
Do the hairy bipedal
hominid stomp!

You got a hairy body
Ain't no dough boy;
Ain't clumsy or cloddy.

Get those big flat feet
on the ground. Let *Homo s.*
hear you beller, hoot, and holler.

Bang a log on a tree;
paradiddle on yer belly.
Let 'em know you're really smelly

but sincere. Haven't bathed
in half a year. Got some nits
but check out these riddem bits.

Gonna get down in the bog,
bang on a hollow log.
Do the Bigfoot Boogie.

Yeah! Get down
and boogie with me, babe.
Ain't no reason to be shy.

Ain't gonna 'buke or 'buse ya.
I'll shave; I'll bathe; amuse ya.
Yeah. C'mon! Get down now!

Put that dainty little foot out,
Yeah, twist it some and shout
You're doin' the bipedal, babe!

Wave yer arms about
And repeat after me;
Do the hairy bipedal hominid stomp.

Ain't Romper Room ready, maybe,
but with a whiff of me, it's heady.
Do the hairy bipedal hominid stomp!

Stomp a little to the left.
Stomp a little to the right.
Shuffle some and boogaloo.

Yer doin it! Yer doin' it!
The hairy bipedal hominid stomp.
The hairy bipedal hominid stomp!

Five SciFaiku, One Tanka

no intelligent life
on this planet to report
Bigfoot boards his craft

✻

All the brochures brag
"selfies with serpent here!"
Champ got no memo

✻

The greys hard at work
at CRISPR cloning cryptids
shoulda stopped at reptiles

✻

sphinx on Mars! You mean
the visitors wanted us
to think one was ours?

✻

Mugwump's stumped –
Lake Tamiskaming for lunch
or hang up his humps?

✻

Monkeyman
hangs near school monkey-bars
no better place
to hang, drain, and skin kids
before he scarfs their innards

Acknowledgments

Poems in this collection have previously appeared in issues of the following e-zines, magazines, journals, and anthologies:

AHF Magazine, Altered Reality, Bewildering Stories, Black Petals, Devour, The Flying Saucer Poetry Review, Granfalloon, Illumen, New Pop Lit (print anthology *Fun Pop Poetry*), *ParAbnormal Magazine, SciFaikuest, The Starlight SciFaiku Review, Trouble Among the Stars,* and *Woolgathering Review.*

Seven SciFaiku appeared in *The Heiligen Effect: Selected Haikai Poems and Sequences* (Ekstasis Editions, 2015)

My thanks to the various editors for their support of the project.

About the Author

Richard Stevenson recently retired to Nanaimo, B.C., from a thirty-year gig teaching English and Creative Writing for Lethbridge College in southern Alberta. He holds an honours BA in English from the University of Victoria and an MFA in Creative Writing from the University of British Columbia and is the author of forty books. Other works in the cryptid critter, ET, and unexplained phenomena series include *Why Were All the Werewolves Men?* (Thistledown Press, 1994), *Nothing Definite Yeti* (Ekstasis Editions, 1999), and *Take Me To Your Leader!* (Bayeux Arts Inc., 2003). Forthcoming are several other collections in the series: *An Abominable Swamp Slob Named Bob* and a trilogy, *Cryptid Shindig* (including the volumes *Frankenfish, Nightcrawlers,* and *Radioactive Frogs*). He has also performed many of the poems with three incarnations of a band called Sasquatch.

About the Illustrator

Carla Stein's illustrations and poetry appear in chapbooks, anthologies, in journals and on walls. You can find her visual work in publications that include *Eye to Eye with My Octopi* (Cyberwit.net, 2022), *The Belladonna, Sad Girl Review, Friday's Poems, Stonecoast Review,* and *The Starlight Scifaiku Review.* Stein's poetry appears in *NonBinary Review, Sustenance* (Anvil Press, 2017), and *Please Hear What I'm Not Saying* (Fly on the Wall Press, 2018) among others. Her illustrated chapbook, *Warp and Weft,* is forthcoming from Tigerpetal Press. Stein is an associate member of the League of Canadian Poets and the current artistic director of Wordstorm Society of the Arts. She makes art and writes poems from her home in Nanaimo, B.C. View her artwork at **www.roaeriestudio.com**

www.ingramcontent.com/pod-product-compliance
Lightning Source LLC
Chambersburg PA
CBHW071159300726
48975CB00004B/1212